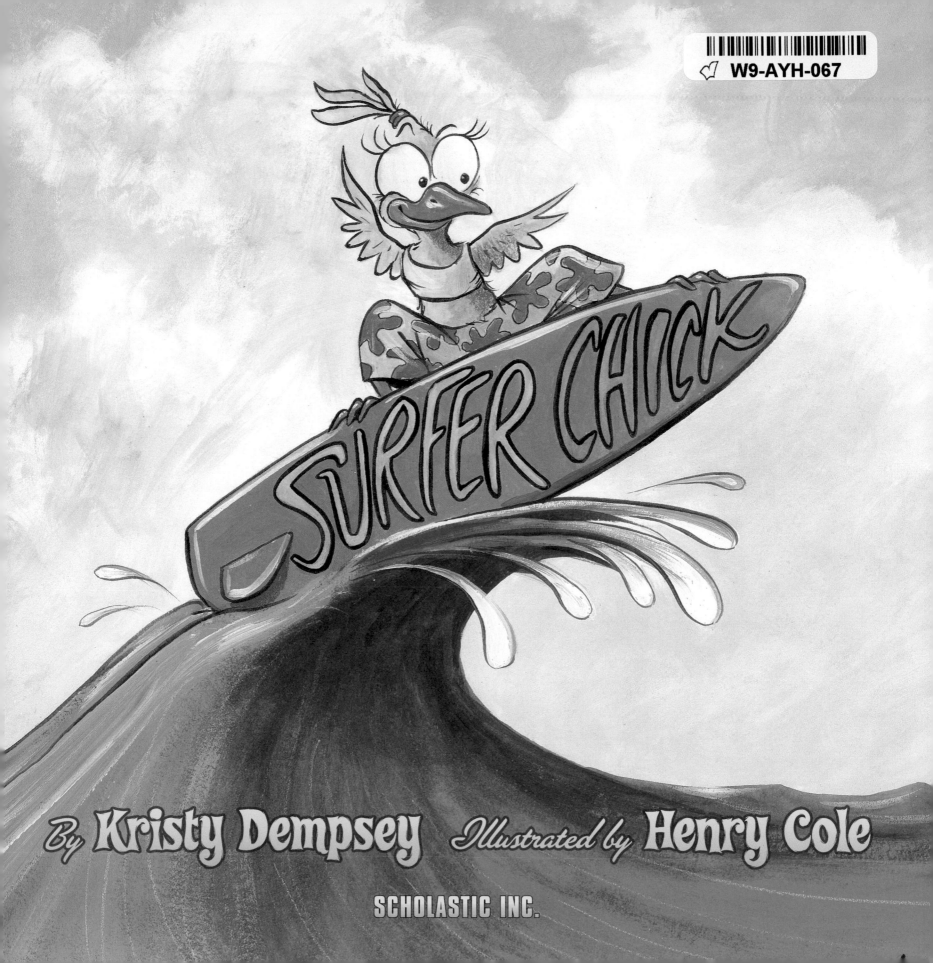

SURFER CHICK

By Kristy Dempsey Illustrated by Henry Cole

SCHOLASTIC INC.

THE ART IN THIS BOOK WAS CREATED
USING ACRYLIC PAINTS AND COLORED PENCILS
ON HOT PRESS WATERCOLOR PAPER.

ISBN 978-0-545-60595-3

Text copyright © 2012 by Kristy Dempsey.
Illustrations copyright © 2012 by Henry Cole.
All rights reserved. Published by Scholastic Inc., 557 Broadway, New York, NY 10012,
by arrangement with Abrams Books for Young Readers, an imprint of Harry N. Abrams, Inc.
SCHOLASTIC and associated logos are trademarks and/or
registered trademarks of Scholastic Inc.

12 11 10 9 8 7 6 5 4 3 2 1   13 14 15 16 17 18/0

Printed in the U.S.A.   08

First Scholastic printing, May 2013

Book design by Maria T. Middleton

For my totally radical niece, Krissy Wike,
who lets me borrow her board
—K. D.

For Tamar, editor, friend,
and surfer chick extraordinaire
—H. C.

Two birds of a feather—
a chick and her dad—
lived by the shore
in a radical pad.

A legend in surfing,
Chick's dad ruled the Roost.
Her dream was to learn
every move he produced.

"I hatched on the beach, dude.
The ocean's my turf.
I swim like a duck.
Will you teach me to surf?"

So Chick and her dad
bought a shiny new board.
It was just the right size,
in a pink Chick adored.

Chick climbed on her board
to learn how to paddle.

But what happened next
was a foul-tempered battle.

Dad floated with Chick and said,

"You'll get the knack.

Just pull with each wing

from the front to the back."

"Now, hop to your feet
and stand up. But there's more:
Steady yourself,
then aim for the shore."

Chick practiced, then . . .
BUMMER! A breaker arose
that ruffled her feathers
and tangled her toes.

It scrambled her focus
and filled her with doubt,

then slung her to shore—
a colossal wipeout.

Alone on the sand,

Chick simply felt chicken.

She rested on shore

till her courage could thicken.

Chick watched her dad surf.
He was ripping along.
His movements were righteous,
so fearless and strong.

Chick copied Dad's moves,
and her confidence soared.
She took a deep breath,
then snatched up her board.

Chick scoped out the water
to find the best wave.
It swelled up behind her . . .
She chose to be brave.

On a wing and a prayer,
with a paddle and splash . . .
Chick popped up and shred
toward the shore in a flash.

She slid through the water
with natural skill,

then added a stunt—
a one-footed thrill!

"I knew you could do it!"
Dad crowed to his chick.
"And all on one foot!
Can you teach me that trick?"

These days when you pass
by the shore near the Roost,
a gnarly new legend
has been introduced.

She's fearless and plucky.
She's stoked and she's quick.
She's totally awesome—
a real Surfer Chick!